Truck Pals on the Job

Hitch Takes Off

written and illustrated by Ken Bowser

RED
CHAIR
•PRESS•™

Funny Bone Readers and Funny Bone Books are published by Red Chair Press
Red Chair Press LLC   PO Box 333   South Egremont, MA 01258-0333
www.redchairpress.com

For my Grandson, Liam Hayden Bowser
who never met a truck he didn't like.

Publisher's Cataloging-In-Publication Data
Bowser, Ken.

  Hitch takes off / written and illustrated by Ken Bowser.

   pages : illustrations ; cm. -- (Funny bone readers. Truck pals on the job)

   Summary: Hitch spends every day moving big planes from around the world into
place at the airport. Will his desire to see the world be fulfilled or will Hitch be left to his
imagination?

   Interest age level: 004-008.

   ISBN: 978-1-63440-071-8 (library hardcover)

   ISBN: 978-1-63440-072-5 (paperback)

   Issued also as an ebook. (ISBN: 978-1-63440-073-2)

   1. Trucks--Juvenile fiction. 2. Airports--Equipment and supplies--Juvenile fiction.
3. Perseverance (Ethics)--Juvenile fiction. 4. Friendship--Juvenile fiction. 5. Trucks--
Fiction. 6. Airports--Equipment and supplies--Fiction. 7. Perseverance (Ethics) -Fiction.
8. Friendship--Fiction. I. Title.

PZ7.B697 Hi 2016

[E]   2015938003

Printed in the United States of America
Distributed in the U.S. by Lerner Publisher Services. www.lernerbooks.com

1015 1P WRZSP16

It was a busy shift at the International Airport. The job of an Airport Pushback Tractor was a tough one and Hitch was the best!

3

He worked very hard every day as he pushed the big jumbo jets to and from their gates and out onto the taxiway. There he waved goodbye to them.

"Au revoir, Monsieur Hitch!"
"Adiós, Señor Hitch." "Sayonara, Mister
Hitch," they would wave back. Hitch
thought about all of the interesting
places the planes were going.

During his lunch break Hitch would listen
to the men and women in the control
tower as the planes prepared for takeoff.

"Flight 909 to Japan, take off!"
"Flight 248 to Mexico, enter the
runway." "Flight 922 to France, leave
your gate," the controller would echo.

Hitch often wondered what it would be like to fly in an airplane and make friends in foreign lands.

"I bet I'd meet all kinds of interesting Pushback Tractors," he thought. "One day I'm going to do it!" said Hitch. "One day I'll go! Yes I will!" he cheered.

"You'll never do it!" chuckled the luggage cart. "Planes are not for tractors! Planes are for passengers." "Impossible!" sneered the food truck. "You'll never go anywhere!"

"You can forget about that!" the fuel truck laughed to Hitch. "You can't go on an airplane. The doors aren't even big enough for a tractor like you," he joked.

Hitch asked the 747 leaving for Italy.
"I am sorry, Signore Hitch," he said.
"I have no room for a tractor. Perhaps
you shall visit Rome, another day."

He asked the giant 767 headed to
China. "Can I come along?" he asked.
"I am sorry, Mister Hitch. Not this
time," she said. "Ask the Airbus.
He is very big."

Airbus was going to England. "Can I come, sir?" Hitch asked. "Sorry, old chap! My doors aren't made for tractors, mate. Ask the Dreamliner! Tallyho!" he said.

Dreamliner was BIG and on her way to France! "Hi," Hitch squeaked. "Can I come?" "I have no room for a tractor. Perhaps another day, mon ami," she said.

"I don't think I'll ever get to see a foreign land or even fly on an airplane," he thought. "I've asked everyone and I've tried as hard as I can," he sighed.

Hitch grew tired and found a big shady
spot for a short nap. "Will I ever get
to ride in an airplane?" he wondered.
"Will I ever see a foreign land?"

Hitch was startled by a thundering
voice. "Who's sleeping on the job while
I am in charge?" the voice ROARED.
"Why, it's just me, sir. Hitch!" he said.

"I'm Colonel Pappy!" the voice roared. "You're sleeping under the biggest cargo plane in the US Air Force!" he rumbled. "On your wheels, soldier!"

Hitch jumped up! This was the biggest
plane ever! "I'm sorry, sir!" Hitch said.
"I just wanted to ride on an airplane
and make friends in other lands."

"I wanted to see the places that all of the planes get to see. It didn't work out today but someday it will! Someday I'll go. I know I will! Don't count me out."

"I like your style, kid!" the huge plane
laughed. "Climb aboard, Hitch. Find
a spot. I'll show you THE WORLD!"
Colonel Pappy laughed. "We can
use a go-getter like you on our air
cargo bases."

Hitch said goodbye to his friends.
Finally, he was riding in an airplane
and he would see all of the places
he had dreamed about. It was an
awesome day for Hitch!

Big Questions: Have you ever imagined meeting new friends in faraway places? Do you think Hitch was happy to meet Colonel Pappy? Why or why not?

Big Words:

controller: a person who gives directions

foreign: strange and unfamiliar

taxiway: where aircraft go when moving to or from a runway